DAN
AND THE
DEAD

THOMAS TAYLOR

QUICKSILVER

First published 2012 by
A & C Black, an imprint of Bloomsbury Publishing Plc
50 Bedford Square, London WC1B 3DP

www.bloomsbury.com
www.acblack.com

ISBN 978-1-4081-5412-0

A CIP catalogue for this book is available from the British Library.

Printed by CPI Group (UK), Croydon, CR0 4YY

1 3 5 7 9 10 8 6 4 2

CONTENTS

For Robert and Rikke

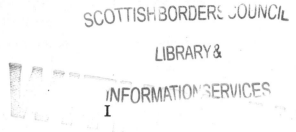

I

MY INVISIBLE WATSON

I'm like that kid. You know, the one in the film who says, 'I see dead people.'

Only I'm not an actor. And the people I see, well, they're not part of some script. They're real.

And yup – they're dead.

For a long time it was scary. And I mean pooing-my-pants scary. When I first realised I was the only one who could see the shapes in my room at night, the only one who could hear them, yeah, I was pretty uncool about it. My parents thought it was nightmares. The doctors thought it was something else and gave me pills. No one believed me, so I'm guessing it's pretty rare what I can do.

Anyway, dead scary – the endless chatter, the reaching hands, the staring 'help me!' eyes. I suppose I was headed for the loony bin. But then something happened a couple of years back, around my twelfth birthday.

I met Simon.

Simon's one of them too – a dead person, I mean – but he's the one who made me realise that I was looking at things the wrong way round. Because yeah, okay, the people who haunt me are *dead*, but they're something else too. They're still people. People who need my help. And when people need something, people will always pay.

Simon's a bit of a mystery though. When the dead linger it's because they've left something undone or unsaid, or because they want revenge, and boy, do they go on about it! But Simon's the first one I've met who's keeping his problems to himself. He's been dead so long, perhaps he can't even remember.

Or perhaps it's because someone put a musket ball through his brain.

Anyway, Simon sticks to me and keeps the other spooks in line, making sure I can get a bit of normal life during the day. Then at midnight (when else?), the interviews start. It's like I'm a psychic private eye or something, only I don't have candles or anything cheesy like that. Simon brings me the desperate dead, one at a time, and I see what I can do for them. Then, if I can help, they give me something very special in return.

You'll find out what later.

And what does Simon get out of all this? I honestly don't know. He just likes to help, I suppose. It's like he's my main ghost.

Hey, everyone wants to feel important.

2

YEAH, SIMON REALLY DOES TALK LIKE THAT

'Si, are you there?'

'Yes, Master Dyer,' comes the silky voice, and I spot Simon in the corner of my room. It's odd how they just appear like that, but I'm used to it.

'Got anything for me tonight?'

'Naturally. You have a sizeable waiting list, though the dead are nothing if not patient. Excepting the old magician, of course. Mr Lugubrian's been demanding to see you again. He has found out about your school show.'

'Si, I've explained,' I say, and not for the first time. 'Lugubrian's a psycho. I'm not doing what he wants, and that's flat. And I wouldn't be seen dead at the school show. Bring me someone else.'

'Someone more your own time, Daniel?'

I sit on my beanbag and turn up the music. I don't want my parents thinking I'm talking to myself again.

'Yeah, hit me.'

There's a moment when nothing happens, then Simon's there again, and now there's someone else there too. I hear a gasp and a high spectral cry, and I dig my fingernails into my hands because it's still a bit scary, all this. A figure runs into the room and stops dead still in front of me, staring down with a ghastly look.

She's about my age, or she was, and even with the terror and fury of the wronged dead twisting her face, I can tell she was quite a looker. Don't take that the wrong way – I just wish I'd met her before, that's all. I often feel like that.

'You can see me?' she shrieks. 'Well, *can* you?'

'Woah, calm down,' I reply, trying to sound like

it's all under control. 'Just take a deep breath and tell me your name. I'm here to help.'

'A deep breath? I'm dead, you moron! *Dead*!' And then she's off again, wailing and rolling her eyes. I'm guessing it hasn't been very long.

'What music do you like?' I have to ask a few times to get her attention. 'I'm online right now. You can have anything you want. Be my guest.'

As I thought, that hits home. The dead can't do much for themselves, so my DJ act usually gets 'em misty-eyed and nostalgic. And quiet.

'Got any Justin Bieber?'

I try not to pull a face – this is business, after all – and tap in the name. Bieber's pretty-boy mug appears on the screen and I click play. The girl stops swooping around and tips her head to one side. The music (if you can call it that) picks up and I can see the girl's remembering. Boy, am I glad ghosts can't cry.

'Daniel, this is Emeline Parker,' says Simon. 'She's only been with us a little while, but I think she's a priority case. It appears to be murder, but I have been unable to obtain details. I've never seen her this calm before.'

'Hi, Ems,' I say, keeping up the professional tone.

'Would you like to tell me? My colleague and I can sort stuff out for people in your, er, situation.'

'I'm dead.' Ems doesn't need to keep saying this, but they usually do. 'And I *so* don't want to be.'

'I know, Ems, I can tell.' I'm genuinely sympathetic – I wouldn't want to be dead either. 'How did it happen? *Was* it murder?'

'Yes. *No*! Well... if you must know, I suppose it's all my own fault.' She looks terrible as she says this. 'But he killed me! No matter what it says in the papers.'

'I see,' I say, even though I don't. Dead or alive, girls are complicated. 'Murder weapon?'

'Bus,' she says, and when she catches me looking all 'say what?' she turns her side to me, and I see it.

She's definitely a bit flatter round the middle than she should be.

But I'm not in the mood for Cluedo so I give her another 'I see,' just for appearances, and glance at the screen. There's plenty of Bieber still to go (professional, Dan, be professional) so I put on my best bedside manner and say, 'Why don't you start at the beginning?'

3

MURDER BY PUBLIC TRANSPORT

E ms is – *was* – like a million other girls in London. Well, okay, a bit better-looking than most, but what I mean is, she's like your sister or your mate's girlfriend or the popular one at school: full of life and drama and shopping. At midnight she should be with her friends having a good time, not standing in my room telling me how she died.

But there's this man in the middle of it all. His name's Carl Bagport, and Carl has a nightclub and a criminal network to run, starting with organised shoplifting and going down from there.

'But why did you do it in the first place?' I think I know the answer, but I need to hear it from her.

'Money.' Ems looks wretched. 'He pays a lot for... well, it's stealing. That's against the law, you know.'

I know.

Simon makes a noise like he's clearing his throat – even though he no longer has one – and I let him speak.

'Forgive me, but I'm not sure I quite understand. You say Mr Bagport was using a photographic apparatus to make pictures of you, Emeline? Doing "shoplifting". But to what end?'

Simon's not quite on the ball when it comes to the twenty-first century. I think he goes back to the eighteenth or something.

'It was just a bit of fun at first. You can pinch things pretty easily if you don't mind the risk. But he started taking orders from his friends, for antiques and stuff. It just got bigger and bigger. Turns out I was good at it.'

'I see,' I say, making a mental note of this for later on. 'So why didn't you quit?'

Ems slumps to the floor and I can see I've got to the nub of it all.

'The pictures he took of me, you know, stealing? Well, he said he'd send them to the police. And my mum and dad. Called it his "insurance". So I had to keep stealing for him, even though he stopped paying me, but then he got pictures of that too. I couldn't get away from him. He said I had to do whatever he told me... then, that last time, I was spotted in Selfridges by a security guard. I ran out into the street, but...'

This must be where the bus comes in.

'It's okay, Ems,' I say, sensing another wailing fit coming on. I wish I could put my arm round her, but you can only comfort a ghost with words.

'Those photos.' Ems is whispering now. 'If my mum had seen them... and my dad – I was his princess – it would have broken his heart.'

Sounds like it already has, I think to myself, and there's actually a lump in my throat because of the stupid tragedy of it all, but there's no time for all that now.

'Listen, here's what happens next, Ems. We need to know everything you know about this Bagport, so we can eliminate him.' I like saying that, 'eliminate him', but I'm just thinking of turning him over to the police – there are enough ghosts about already. 'But first, there's just the little matter of payment.'

Em's head snaps up and her eyes lock mine. Whoops! Bad timing, Dan.

'What do you think I can give you?' Ems is not happy. In fact, she's flaming mad and her ghost's all fierce and flickery. 'God, you're just like him! All you men are the same!'

'Wait, Ems.' I'm holding my hands up like she has a gun or something. I need to make her feel strong again, so she'll listen. 'It's not what you think.'

She's upright now, and her eyes are like the business end of a double-barrelled tank, but at least she's stopped shouting.

'It's not what you think.' I say again. 'Simon and me, we don't expect money or anything, we just need a little favour from you. We'll help you get even, and do our best to put Carl Bagport out of business for good. In return, before you move on to the Hereafter, I just need...'

And I tell her. It's the same deal I offer them all, and like the others she just stares at me in amazement. Then she laughs.

'Is that even possible?'

I nod and smile back.

It looks like a done deal to me.

4

THE GENTLEMAN OF MIRACLES

T he thing about school is, even top paranormal investigators have to go there if they're only fourteen. You'd think Ems would understand this, but when I tell her that hunting down Bagport's going to have to wait till after Geography, History and a visit from a fireman, she's not best pleased.

She even trails me out of the house, moaning, despite Simon's best efforts to clear the decks for the day. It's only when the school bus wheezes up that I lose her.

I suppose she's got a thing about buses now.

There's one good side to school though: there aren't any ghosts there. Simon sees to that. And anyway it's so new that no one's died there yet, despite the dodgy smells that hang around the canteen. So it's just the living at school, though, yeah, some of the teachers are dead boring. Especially Mr Harris. History Harris is so deathly dull he turns kids into zombies.

'Today we shall discuss the Congress of Vienna and its long-term impact on Franco-German relations,' drones the Harris, and I tune out while I still can. I'm drawing skulls in my exercise book, thinking about poor Ems, when something makes me look up. A shape is looming. Why do shapes do that?

'Pick a card,' creaks a voice I dread almost more than the Harris's, and there, standing in front of me, is the scraggy spirit of Mr Lugubrian, rigged out like Count Dracula in the get-up he died in. 'Go on, boy, *pick one*!' And he leers at me through his whiskers, fanning a deck of enormous ghostly playing cards.

'Buzz off,' I manage to hiss without drawing too much attention. 'You know what Si'll do if he catches you here.'

'Bah! I'm not scared of Bullet Brain,' says Mr Lugubrian, and he snaps the cards shut in a puff of ectoplasm. 'But I am most displeased with you, boy. How dare you let that strumpet jump the queue? I demand you address my affairs first.'

'Ems is no strumpet,' I say, making a mental note to ask Si what 'strumpet' means, but it seems I spoke too loudly, because everyone turns to stare at me. The room is silent. The Harris pulls his specs down his nose and stares hardest of all.

'Do you wish to say something about trumpets, Daniel, or are you talking to yourself again?'

Laughter ripples round the room and a ball of paper bounces off my head. Yup, I have a certain reputation.

'No, sir.'

'Then kindly shush.' The Harris's mouth is as tight as a cat's bum. 'Now, class, turn to page 879...'

In the rustling that follows, I hiss at the ghost of the Victorian magician to get lost, but the old man knows he's got me cornered. Where the hell's Si?

'They laughed at me too,' Lugubrian says, the purple bags under his eyes quivering. 'Afterwards. They said I was nothing but a penny conjuror, a rabbit worrier, a... a... *vaudevillian*! Me! Just because that last trick went awry. But I was Silas Lugubrian, Gentleman of Miracles! Lugubrian's "Head-in-his-hands" Illusion should have been the wonder of the age!' and he rolls his head at me.

Literally.

It's always the same thing with old Gubie. He died 130 years ago, performing a magic trick of his own invention in front of a live audience. It's a cage with a couple of spring-loaded blades at neck height, a cage you put over your head. Can you guess where this is going? Yup, that's right. Anyway, at least it was named well, the trick. Lugubrian's 'Head-in-his-hands' Illusion did indeed leave Gubie's very own head in his very own hands. Along with a lot of his very own blood.

'But you can help me, boy.' Lugubrian's getting into his stride now. He's stalking his invisible way round the classroom like a hunchbacked spider, one hand fixed behind his back, the other gesturing in the air, while his head bobs up and down on his shoulders. There are flashes of daylight where his neck should be. 'You *must* help!'

'No,' I manage to cough, and the Harris glances at me.

'Dig up the apparatus!' Lugubrian turns on his heel

and delivers his words at me like he's back on stage. 'Make the adjustments! Perform my trick for me, so that the name of Silas Lugubrian can live down the ages!'

And it would take ages to live down a name like that, I think, but out loud I hiss, 'Stop yabbering, you stupid old codger!' Only I shouldn't hiss this, should I? Because now everyone's staring at me again.

'Daniel Dyer, on your feet!' shouts History Harris, and Mr Lugubrian, unseen by everyone but me, spreads his mouth into a hook-tooth grin. Me? All I can do is stand up.

'Yabbering, am I?' The Harris is closing in like an elderly knight in corduroy armour. '*Old codger*, am I? How dare you?'

'Sir, I wasn't talking to you, sir,' is the best I can do, because all I'm thinking is how I'd kill Simon if he wasn't already dead. Where is he?

'Woooh!' go a load of voices around me, and 'There's a ghost!' Even the Harris chuckles along. There are some things you just don't live down at school, and talking to people who aren't there's pretty high on the list.

'All right, Daniel.' You can tell Mr Harris thinks he's got me. And this time, perhaps he has. 'Before

I give you a month's detention, you have one last chance. Let's see if your invisible friends can help you answer a question about the Treaty of Vienna. When was it signed?'

Well, I haven't a clue, have I? But you can tell old Gubie has by the way his head somersaults. Then, with the hand that isn't always behind his back, he plucks his head off its stump and flings it, top hat and all, to where I stand sweating in front of Harris.

'Spot of bother, boy?' the head croons in one ear. 'Need old Silas to help you out?' it simpers in the other.

I shake my head very, very slightly. There's no way I'm sticking the old brain box in Lugubrian's death-trap apparatus just to avoid detention, but at the same time, I need to get out after school to help Ems.

The Harris leans closer. 'Well?'

I'm in a pickle, though I won't lose my head over it. But what's Ems gonna say?

Lugubrian's grin presses closer and closer, his blood-filled eyes glowing red with glee.

'Dig up the apparatus! Perform my trick at your wretched school show! I'll tell you the answer if you do…'

And that's when, finally, Simon arrives. He cries 'Zooks!' when he spots what's going on.

I roll my eyes his way and give him one of my 'where-in-Death's-name-have-you-been' looks. The Harris is about to start shouting when Simon speaks rapidly into my ear. Detention is heading my way, but thanks to Si I can now deflect it.

'The Treaty of Vienna was signed on the 25th of March, 1815,' I shout out, repeating Simon's words. 'Unless you mean the treaty of 1809. That was signed on the 14th of October. There are eight other treaties with that name. I can, er, probably tell you when they were signed too. If you like.'

The Harris is speechless. So is everyone else. Except Simon that is, who's yelling 'Poltroon! Pox-monger!' at old Gubie and using the magician's own head to swat his crooked, black ghost-body as it runs here and there, trying to escape.

But only I can see that.

The bell goes then, and the other kids can't get out of the room fast enough. They laugh at me, sure, but enough strange stuff goes on when I'm in the room to make sure they only laugh from a safe distance. I stroll out of the class like I don't care. It's only when we're in the toilets that I really let rip at Simon.

'I apologise.' He bows when he says this, so I think he probably means it. 'But I thought it would save time if I spent the day following the scoundrel Bagport.'

Something about his voice makes me forget Lugubrian. Simon looks furious, and small angry clouds of ectoplasm are puffing out of the hole in his head like he's a steam train.

'I found him,' says Si, 'and it's not just Emeline. Bagport has dozens of young people in his employ, forced to commit crimes for him. He trades in misery, Daniel. We must act tonight!'

5

SIMON'S PARTY TRICK

It's after school and getting dark, and I'm strolling along with Simon drifting beside me. Obviously I'm the only one who can see him. Ems hasn't reappeared yet, but it's only a matter of time. Meanwhile, Simon and me, we've got work to do.

I'm wearing my black leather coat. It's not a biker's one, it's an antique from the 70s, and very long. It wasn't me who Tippexed skulls all over it, honest. I also have purple-tinted sunglasses and a china false eye on a chain round my neck. This isn't how I always dress, you understand, but it sure does help put the wind up my victims if I go a bit Gothic and creepy.

In my pocket there's a USB memory stick, but more about that soon.

We're in a pretty rough part of town, on our way to Bagport's club, but Simon's already checked the place out and he's as cool as a cucumber. About as cheerful as one too.

The thing about Simon is that he's like a cross between a butler on the one hand, and an all-out nut job on the other. One minute he's all, 'Yes, sir. No, sir. Don't believe it's so, sir.' Then the next, something'll happen – like finding Lugubrian at my school – and he just blows up like a demon psycho from the inner circle of Hell.

Mostly though, it's the cucumber.

'Zooks, Daniel! I can't believe how little has changed since my day,' he says, and I roll my purple eyes. 'Thievery, poverty, the rich using their power to exploit the poor. What happened to Emeline has been happening in one form or another since biblical times.'

'Blimey, Simon – cheer up, mate.'

I'm not in the mood for another one of his speeches.

'Yours may be an age of wonders, Daniel, but the human condition is as miserable now as it ever was.'

'All right, keep your wig on,' I say. I often say this because Simon actually has a wig on, one of those powdery jobs with a ponytail. Imagine going through eternity looking like that! 'Let's stop moaning about it and do our bit to make the world a better place.'

We turn into a back alley and stop beside a rusty metal door. According to Si, this is the back of Carl Bagport's club. It smells bad enough for a scumbag's dive at any rate. I try the door but of course it's locked.

'Allow me,' says Simon, and he reaches into the lock and does his party trick.

Mostly the dead are completely helpless, but Simon's been around a few hundred years and he's learnt a thing or two. There's a slight scraping from inside the lock, and then a satisfying 'slunk' as the barrels tumble. Simon turns and bows low. I do one half of a high five all by myself – don't worry, no one's watching – and then open the door.

Inside it's about as scuzzy as it can get. There are boxes of crisps and booze, all damp and collapsing, and a manky armchair in one corner surrounded by about a million fag ends and crushed beer cans. On the other side is a door, but this time Simon's not needed.

Outside in the corridor there's stairs going up, and here the red carpet begins. I creep up, silent on my fat heels, and stick my head round the door at the top. The room inside is all mirrors and gold gilt and plush furnishings, and no end of shiny knick-knacks. It's like a French lady's boudoir, only with a strong smell of Eau de Wide Boy aftershave and cigarettes. And I hear voices.

There's a man behind an enormous white desk, his feet up and his hands behind his head. Bagport. His tan's so fake he's almost orange, and his hair's as golden as the horrible furniture. He's talking at some scared-looking kid standing opposite him. I reckon he's a bit younger than me, this kid. He's emptying his pockets while Bagport's yacking on about being Mr Big, but I haven't come here to be a spectator. I walk straight in.

'Barbie's on the phone,' I say, looking round the glitzy room, 'and she wants her stuff back.'

There's a moment of astonished silence, then our man Bagport's on his feet.

'What the…?' he shouts. 'Who are you? How the hell did you get in here?'

'I've come for Emeline,' I say, and he looks at me like I'm crazy.

'Emeline? You mean that stupid bint who went under a bus? Give me a break!'

But I don't give him a break. I give him one of my special mystic looks and place my fingertips together. I can see he's about to start shouting again, so I give him my 'I see dead people' speech too.

He's not impressed.

'Get out of here now, kid, or the only dead person round here will be you.'

They usually say something like this, and it's Simon's cue to get busy. Peering over my purple glasses I lift my hand and point at Bagport's head, like I'm Darth Vader or something. Simon, who has taken up his invisible position just behind the desk, reaches one ghostly hand into Bagport's neck and applies the same pressure that opened the lock to close the blood vessels to the man's brain. It only takes a moment before Mr Big's reaching for his head and gasping. Then he's out cold on the floor, a look of disbelief frozen on his face.

The kid's out of the room in like one second flat.

'Shame you weren't here to see that, Ems,' I say. 'But I'm saving the best till last.'

Then I step over Bagport's sleeping body, sit down at the desk, and fire up his computer.

6

THE FIRING PIN QUESTION

It's not going at all badly until it goes totally wrong.

I'm sitting there at Bagport's computer, hacking past his feeble security measures, crawling all over his hard drive like a monkey on a cupcake, when I hear a click behind me. And it's a shame, that click, because it's all there: photos, orders, and enough incriminating evidence to make sure Bagsy gets busted big style. Yeah, some of the kids he's got working for him'll get into hot water too, but that's what Social Services are for, right? I mean, they're *kids*. Anyway, there I am, downloading the lot, when I hear that click.

It's Bagport. They almost never wake up as quick as that, and it's a pity Bagport does, because the man's only got a gun, hasn't he?

'Geagh…' he says, struggling to focus, but with his gun pointed right at me. That probably means 'stick 'em up' or something – we all watch the same TV – so I lean back from the keyboard and stick 'em up as high as I can. Well, I'm not stupid, am I? I glance over at Simon, but Si's gone whiter than a seagull dropping, and he's hopping from one foot to another in old-fashioned distress, saying 'Zooks!' over and over.

If I'm Batman, then Si's definitely Robin.

Bagport coughs his voice back as he stands, keeping the gun on me all the time. Then he lunges forward, pressing it into the back of my head.

'You snivelling little runt!' he spits out. 'I don't know how you did that, but I'm gonna make you wish you hadn't.'

Obviously, this is when Ems decides to drop in and see how the dynamic duo's getting on.

'What's happening?' she says, then she stops, amazed at the sight before her. 'Oh.'

Simon's too busy chewing his wig to speak, so it's up to me to reassure our client.

'S'okay, Ems,' I manage to get out, even though my cheek's pressed into the computer screen. 'S'all under control.'

'What kind of sicko are you?' Bagport's hand is shaking now, which means his trigger finger'll be getting twitchy too. 'There's no one here!' And then he seems to realize something, and chuckles darkly. 'Hey, who knows that *you're* here?'

I glance at Si, and Si looks back. I know exactly what's going on in his mind.

You see, we've been over this whole question time and again, me and Si. What if someone pulled a gun on me? Would it be curtains for our hero? Or would Si be quick enough with his party trick to stop the firing pin? Simon's always said 'Yes, probably, yes,' and yes is a good answer.

It's the 'probably' part that bothers me.

But I know and Si knows that he's already done his trick twice in the last few minutes, and whatever spooky battery Si uses to move stuff with his mind gets flat pretty quick. And a gun's a gun, after all. Right now, I'm guessing I can't even count on 'probably'.

Looks like it's up to me.

'Now, Mr Bagport,' I say. 'Don't go making another ghost. I'd've thought having Ems haunting you'd be enough.'

'Oh, cut the crap,' says Bagport. 'Who sent you?'

'It's Ems. I told you. She's standing right there.' And I manage to tip my head towards the part of the room where Simon is still wringing his ghostly hands and Ems is shaking her head like she knew I was a doofus all along. I don't like her looking at me like that, but I'm too busy noticing something else to really mind: the memory stick is still in the computer, and I don't think Bagport's spotted it. Yet. I've got to keep him talking.

'Emeline!' I cry, in my spookiest voice. 'Give us a sign!'

The ghost of Ems puts her hands on her hips. Instead of a sign she gives me that 'what-have-I-stepped-in?' look girls do so well, but that's okay because it's really Si I'm talking to. And fortunately, Si's finally getting it together.

There's a poncy great chandelier in the centre of the ceiling, and concentrating as hard as he can, Si manages to set it swinging with the last of his spirit powers. As the light turns and the shadows dance weirdly about, I hear Bagport gasp and swear and step back in surprise. I grab the USB stick, yank it out, and stuff it in my shoe.

'Behold, the sign!' I really love doing the spooky voice.

'Impossible!' Bagport's crouching back, waving his gun at the swinging chandelier. 'It's not possible!' But I don't hang around to argue. I'm up and running across the room.

The man shouts after me, swearing like Captain Potty Mouth, and I half expect to hear the gun go off, but I'm banking on him not wanting to make all that noise now, not without the back of my head as a silencer. Instead he's blundering after me as I slide down the banister. When I skid into the storeroom, there's some geezer there, lighting up, but he's not expecting a pale kid in purple glasses and a death's head coat, is he? I barge him down, and then Bagsy trips over him, and before you can say 'scarper' I'm out and pelting down the back alley in a storm of wheelie bins.

It's only when I'm about a mile away and hiding in a skip that I reach into my shoe and find the USB stick's gone.

'Zooking hell!'

7

A GRAVE BUSINESS

'A right pair of numpties, you are!'

It's the next day and we're in the toilets, the ones behind the school swimming pool. No one uses them, except me when I need to talk to Si, only today Ems is there too. And I'm not so worried about being caught talking to myself right now, because with Ems I can hardly get a word in edgeways.

'I wanted revenge!' she's shouting. 'Not Chuckles the clown and his dancing newt! And what does "zooks" mean anyway? No, don't answer that, Frilly Knickers! Just tell me what you're going to do about it. God, if there was only someone else who could see me...'

'Ems,' I say into a gap. 'Ems, it's just a setback! We'll get him, don't worry. It's just going to take a bit longer than we thought, that's all.'

'It was most unfortunate that Bagport was armed,' Simon puts in. 'I should have searched him first. Emeline, please don't be angry with Daniel. The blames lies with me.'

'Okay,' I say, before Ems can throw in any more insults. 'Coolio. I'm thinking the memory stick's still the way forward. It's got everything we need on it. It must've fallen out when I was, er...'

'Running like a chicken in Kentucky?' suggests Ems helpfully.

'A chicken who'll live to cluck another day,' I reply. 'Which is more than I can say for you two. Anyway, I don't think Bagport even knew there *was* a memory stick. We'll go back tonight and look for it.'

'He'll catch you,' Ems says. 'I know him. He won't let this go. If you go back there, he'll catch you.'

'Nah,' I say. 'It's all good. We'll find the stick and send it to the police with a note. The job's as good as jobbed.'

So it's agreed. Well, Ems doesn't have much choice does she, because who else is there? Psychic kids and gentleman ghosts don't exactly advertise in the Yellow Pages.

The meeting breaks up and I'm going back to class super slow (algebra'll do that to your feet) when I turn a corner and come face to face with the Harris. I try and moonwalk back round, but it's no good, he's seen me. That's more than you can say for Mrs Chalmsworth, though. I bump into her coming the other way.

'Be careful!' hoots Mrs C. 'But… oh yes, Daniel Dyer – I've been meaning to talk to you.'

The Harris stops to listen. I've got corduroy to the left of me and drama teacher swirls to the right, and suddenly being shouted at by Ems doesn't seem so bad.

'Is the boy bothering you?' says the Harris, fixing his beady eye on me. But he's out of luck, because probably the only person in the school who isn't bothered by me is Mrs C. Mrs C actually likes me. I wonder if it's the purple glasses.

'Not at all, he's just the person I wanted to see,' she honks in a voice that could bring down light aircraft. 'Now, Daniel, have you had time to consider the school show?'

I have had time to consider it, and I consider that not even a basket of rap star gold and a slice of unicorn pie could get me on stage at the school show. I'm just rounding my lips to say 'No freakin' way,' when the voice sweeps over me again.

'Oh, I'm so glad! I knew I could count on you!'

'But – '

'It's the freestyle slot I'm having the most trouble with. No one wants to go on and improvise, though I can't think why. But a short act with you and your imaginary friends, and perhaps a little trick or two, would be just perfect.'

'Him? On stage?' The Harris is aghast, but a look from Mrs C wipes him out.

'I'll put you down for ten minutes, then. And don't forget, it's this Saturday night, so get your thinking cap on.' And she's off before I can even pick my bottom jaw off the floor.

Do you ever get the feeling that you're not in control of your own life? It's like Fate's got me by the danglies and won't let go. I mean, if Lugubrian's ghost appeared now and slapped me on the back I wouldn't be surprised. But I'm not going to be appearing on stage on Saturday and chopping off my own head in front of the whole school, so Fate and old Gubie can just bog off.

* * *

That evening, after school, I'm back in the alleyways near Bagport's club, retracing my steps and wondering if it's safe to have a bit of a shufty near the bins. I'm pretty sure that's where the stick fell. Si's with me, drifting close to the ground and round behind things where I can't go. I've got a very small torch with a narrow beam, but there's no joy, just loads of bins standing around in the dark and nothing else. The pavement almost feels cleaner than it should be, and it's so quiet that I'm starting to get a bad feeling.

'Any luck?' I whisper to Si.

'Not a bean,' he replies.

I'm just thinking it's time to jack it in for the night, when something happens that gives me the fright of my life. And for a kid who sees dead people, that's saying a lot.

The lid of this wheelie bin I'm next to bursts up, and someone grabs my arm! I yell out and twist my arm in a karate move. It's a good move too, something I picked up from a client, and I break the man's grip easily, but another bin explodes open. Two great bear arms pick me up. I see Simon swoop over and hear him shout 'Daniel!' but before he can get there, I'm being stuffed into a bin like a sack of potato peelings, and the lid slams shut.

Next thing I know, I'm being trundled about and then I'm tipped out on the ground. I try to run, but the same enormous pair of hands grabs me and I'm pushed into the back of a car. The doors slam and the car starts to drive. I sit up, remove a rotten cabbage leaf from my specs and stare back at the sneering face of Carl Bagport.

'Looking for this, were we?'

He's holding a gun in one hand, and the USB stick in the other.

'Zounds!' gasps Simon, who's slipped in beside me.

'Nah, you can keep that,' I say. 'I've got others.'

I'm trying to sound cool about things, even though I'm really, really not. Bagsy grins as he pops the stick into the top pocket of his suit. Then he reaches out to a little tray and picks up a martini glass full of something gloopy and pink.

The car's some naff stretched job with back seats facing each other, and next to Bagport there's a bloke with a camera round his neck, a bloke who looks like the Incredible Hulk's mean uncle. He's holding a gun too. Simon can't do his trick on both men at once, but then I guess that's the point.

'Do you know who this is, Ringpull?' says Bagport to the huge bloke. The huge bloke grunts. 'It's only the kid who sees dead people.'

Ringpull glances over at his boss, and for a moment it almost looks like he has the brains to not believe what he's hearing. But he just grunts again and goes on pointing his pistol. I look back at Bagport and it's a surprise to see the man's looking at me with genuine interest.

'What, you believe me?' I say. I'm not used to this.

'Oh, I don't know yet.' Bagport takes a little sip from his glitzy cocktail, but one of the umbrellas falls out and leaves a sticky trail on his shiny suit. I'm thinking he's trying to give me the Mr Big act with the flash car and everything, but all I can see are some serious style issues. Oh, and guns. I can see those too.

'But what you did to me yesterday – knocking me out, and the swinging chandelier... There's something about you I don't get,' he says. 'But I will, kid, I will. I didn't get to where I am today by turning my back on opportunities, and if you *can* see dead people... well, there's an opportunity that doesn't come along every day.' And he gives me a sick leer. His teeth are even whiter than Simon's.

The car drives for a bit longer, and then pulls up. Outside it's really dark, too dark for London, but in the light that spills from the car doors as they open I spot a crumbly brick wall, a mass of ivy and an ancient iron gate. The gate is open, and there's someone there. I catch a glimpse of the terrified face of a girl, but she runs off when Ringpull cuffs her round the head. There are keys in the gate, and I just know they've been nicked from somewhere, on Bagsy's orders.

I'm pulled out of the car, and then Bagport's next to me, his gun in my back. I can tell he's carrying something else, but I can't see what. He pushes me towards the gate and then, despite the gloom, I clock what's through there.

Gravestones.

Hundreds of gravestones.

With a shove, I'm through the gate and standing amongst them.

'It's Highgate Cemetery,' Simon says in a whisper. 'But what…?' He gets no further than this though because now he's staring behind me with a look of horror on his face.

I turn slowly and in the dark Bagport shoves something heavy at me.

'Okay, kid. You say you can talk to the dead? Well, here's your conversation starter.'

I look at my hands.

I'm holding a spade.

8

THE DEAL
(IF YOU CAN CALL IT THAT)

'I love an antique, me,' says Bagport, as we stroll in the graveyard at night. 'I've got plenty of kids working for me, as you know, but it's the ones who pinch the antiques I value the most.'

I'm just stumping along, two guns trained on me, while Si drifts glumly at my side. At least Ems isn't here to see this.

'But did you know that right here in the city there are unclaimed antiques galore, just lying around, waiting to be picked up?' Bagport waves at the cemetery around us. 'Heh, those Victorians! They all died in the end. And they loved to be buried with their stuff, didn't they, your Victorians? Silver watches, gold monocles, ivory false teeth… who needs to go to Egypt when you can raid tombs right here?'

'You want to dig them up?' I can't help asking. 'But that's mad! There's loads of 'em!'

'I only need one hole tonight, kid.' I can tell Bagport's grinning by the sugar in his voice. We stop walking.

'Here's how things are,' he says. 'You know too much about me and that's not a healthy situation. For you. Now, either you can really talk to the dead, in which case you're valuable because you can ask around the stiffs and find me a coffin with a diamond tiara in it, or…' He grinds the gun into my back. '… or it's all a load of cobblers but at least you'll have dug your own grave, in which case I can leave you here with Ringpull and go home for my kipper. Got it?'

I'll admit that my shoulders are sagging a bit by now. Well, it's not looking good for yours truly, is it?

I turn to Si, and I speak to him out loud, something I never normally do in front of other people. Right now though, there doesn't seem to be any point in secrecy.

'Well, buddy? Any options?'

'Ha, look!' Bagport says to Ringpull. 'He's doing it already!'

Ringpull just grunts at what looks like empty night air to him.

'Daniel.' Simon's talking urgently. 'There's no chance this can work. Even if I can locate a coffin six feet down, there's no way I could see in the dark to tell you what's in it. And while I could probably find a fellow ghost or two hereabouts, they are unlikely to know what they were buried with. It's a mad scheme that can only lead to disappointment. I'm afraid your only option is to flee. I could probably knock one of them out, and perhaps with the dark...'

But I hold my hand up. They've both got torches, they've both got guns. I wouldn't get twenty paces.

'Okay,' I say to Bagport. 'I'll do it.'

'Daniel, no!' Simon wails. 'I cannot help you. He's expecting treasure, but he'll kill you if you dig up nothing!'

But I just nod my head. Fact is, all this talk about

digging stuff up has given me an idea. And if I *do* find something, then Bagport'll count me as one of his kids, won't he? Which means I'll be working for him. And if I'm working for him, then maybe I can find a way to bring him down for Ems. I'll be like the enemy within. Or something. At the very least, I'll live a bit longer, something I'm quite keen on doing, believe me.

But it's a shame I can't say all this to Si, who clearly thinks I've gone mad when I ask Bagport for a torch.

'Follow me,' I say, and I stride off into the graveyard, in search of a dank cheerless grave I've seen once before. The two men stump along close behind me.

We walk for quite a bit because it takes a while to get my bearings, but just as Bagport's starting to lose patience, I stop. I've found it.

I shine the torch across the white stone and the miserable-looking angel carved on top of it. In front there's a broken stone grave slab and a tangle of thorns and nettles. I drive the spade into the ground and turn around.

'Here,' I say. 'There's something valuable buried here.'

'You're sure?' I can tell Bagport's struggling to decide if he's wasting his time or not. 'I didn't hear you talk to anyone.'

I shrug. 'I've chatted to the gentleman buried here many times,' I say, and in the chill quiet of the graveyard at night, I can see both Bagport and Ringpull are rattled by that. They get a bit closer to each other.

'Daniel, are you quite sure about this?' Si's looking toward the gravestone with a hostile eye.

I nod and look too. Across the peeling stone the torchlight picks out the leaden name:

Silas Lugubrian
1815 ~ 1882
Gentleman of Miracles
Master of Illusion, Until The End

And behind the stone, a look of unholy triumph across his sallow features, stands the ghost of the man himself.

'Come to help old Silas, have you, boy?'

9

BURKE AND HARE
HAD IT EASY

In no time at all, Ringpull has dragged the great broken slabs off the grave, and yanked back armfuls of nettles and brambles with his bare hands. Then everyone's looking at me. I can't quite believe what's happening, but I pick up the spade and dig it into the sodden earth anyway. I mean, what else can I do?

I'm two spadefuls in when I realize I'm never going

to dig all that way down on my own. It's a joke, and a sick one at that. I turn to glare at Bagport, poised with my foot driving the spade into the ground, and…

FLASH!

I fall back, dazzled, lifting a clod of mud high with the spade, and…

FLASH!

For a moment I can't see a thing, but then I remember the camera round Ringpull's neck. Bagport's got pictures now, and I'm getting more and more entangled in his web.

I dig a bit more, and the ghost of Silas Lugubrian is standing over me.

'The apparatus!' he's saying, rubbing his hands 'Oh, my apparatus! I knew you would see sense, boy. A few little tweaks and it should work perfectly. I'm almost certain I know what went wrong. You'll be the toast of your school show, and my reputation shall be restored!'

I look up at him.

'I'm not doing this for you,' I snap. 'So don't go getting any ideas. Only an idiot would put their head in your *apparatus* after what happened to you.'

'Kid, are you really talking to the ghost of the man buried here?' says Bagport. I can tell he's intrigued by it all, despite himself, and there's even a tremble in his voice. 'On the level now. What does he look like?'

I stop digging and glance at Lugubrian. The ghost leers at me and makes his ugly whiskery head turn a complete circle. Slowly.

'Be quiet and let me dig,' I say to Bagport.

I'm in a bad mood. But by now it's clear to everyone that I'm going to take all night, and perhaps they're ready for this, because at a word from his boss Ringpull seizes the spade and shoves me to one side. In a moment he's powering down through the earth, flinging great lumps of the stuff out of the deepening hole.

The man's like a digging machine, and all I can do is sit on a fallen stone angel and watch, and hope that all Lugubrian's whining about his 'apparatus' isn't just bull.

It's nearly an hour before we hear the spade 'thunk' into something hard, and I know I'm about to find out.

Bagport stands next to the hole and shines the torch down. For a moment I think I can escape while both men are distracted, but Bagport must think the same thing, because he grabs me.

'Ringpull, get up here!' he says, and before I know it I'm being sent down the hole myself. The spade's still there. In the dry earth at the bottom there's a hole, though what the hole's really in is a wooden panel.

It's the lid of a coffin.

'Get it clear, kid, and get the loot out,' comes Bagsy's voice from above. 'But I warn you, if you've been wasting my time, Ringpull will start chucking the earth back in.

Ringpull grunts.

The idea of being buried alive in the grave of Silas Lugubrian is not one of the highlights of the evening. Simon's standing at the graveside too, his hands clamped firmly on the old magician's ghostly shoulders, but he can't send Lugubrian away now, not from his own patch. In any case, there's nothing Si can do to stop the magician's head from floating down to join me.

'All these years!' says the head, bobbing about. 'All that waiting… finally! Go gently, boy. Oh, my poor old bones! Take the apparatus gently.'

I expose the lid a bit more. Ringpull takes a few more pictures, and I'm imagining what would happen if those shots of yours truly robbing a Victorian tomb ever got shown round the school. Yeah, it'd be a scandal, but you know what? No one'd be too surprised.

'Get on with it!' shouts Bagport.

I smack the spade down on the brittle wood, and a great split spreads down the coffin lid. Inside it's dark, but I can only open the split wood a little way, there's too much earth.

'Put your hand in,' says the sickly voice of Lugubrian. He's enjoying this far too much. 'I *dare* you.'

No freakin' way.

I whack the spade down again and again, and the lip collapses a bit more.

Inside I can see bones. It's the skeleton of Silas Lugubrian, the top half anyway, exposed after well over a century. But there's no sign of anything else buried there, and something's not quite right.

His skull is missing.

Lugubrian's ghostly head looks shocked for a moment, before swooping into the coffin and down towards his own bony feet, which are still out of sight. Then it comes zooming out again, roaring with indignation.

'Blackguards!' Lugubrian shouts. 'The infamy of it!'

Oh, crapsticks, I'm thinking. *There's nothing here after all!*

'Where's your stupid apparatus?' I shout at the head. 'You said it'd be here!' Up at the graveside there's a stony silence as the two men look down at me, their pistols glinting in the torchlight.

'It *is* there, you dolt!' says the ghost. 'Down by my feet, but – '

But I don't want his 'but', I just want out of this stinking hole, so I take a deep breath and reach down into the black of the coffin. I close my hand over a cold metal something, and heave at it with all my strength. For a moment nothing happens, but then, with a crash-splatter of dry earth and wood, I fall back, and the something lands on top of me. It's a mouldy old metal cage thing, about a foot square, with a rusted spring and a lever, all dark green with age and fungus. And there's something inside.

Yup. It's Lugubrian's skull.

JOHNNY SPARKO'S EARACHE

It's one in the morning when I get in, and my parents are furious. Apparently they almost called the police, which might have been a very good thing, though given what I've been up to, perhaps not. I manage to get away in the end and have a shower – I can't think straight with Lugubrian's grave muck under my fingernails. Afterwards, I'm pretty tired, but when I get back to my room, they're standing there, all three of them, waiting for an explanation.

'What?' I say to Si. His arms are folded. So are Em's. The ghost of Silas Lugubrian is fuming with rage and his head has gone into indignant orbit round my light bulb. You'd think he at least would be happy, but instead he's whinging on and on.

'Such an insult! Burying my head at my feet! But I'll have the last laugh. We'll see how they like it when – '

'Oh, be quiet!' Simon shouts, and he bats the head across the room. It vanishes through the wall. The ectoplasm is puffing out of the hole in Si's head again.

'So, you're working for him now?' says Ems, in a voice so controlled it's dangerous. 'Bagport. You're one of his kids. I came to you for help and you've betrayed me.'

Can't they give me a break? I'm in my dressing gown, for crying out loud. But it seems they're not going to let it go till I give a little speech. You know, to rally the troops.

'It's cool,' I say. 'I'm getting close to Bagport. When he lets his guard down, I'll sort him. Then you'll be free, Ems. And Lugubrian, at least you've got part of what you wanted so you can leave me alone now. I doubt I'll get a smile from you, Si, but I'm used to that.'

The magician's head swoops back in and snarls at me from near my ankles, like a whiskery bloodhound.

'You will perform the trick at your school show?'

'Nope,' I say.

'But, Daniel!' cries Simon. 'How can you get close to Bagport? Now he thinks you can find treasure in coffins, he's expecting to go back to the cemetery tonight. I told you, I cannot help you locate treasure there. You happened to know about Lugubrian's apparatus, but what will you tell Bagport next time? What can you possibly dig up tonight?'

'And what's he doing with my priceless apparatus anyway?' barks the head.

'How could you join him? A man like that?' says Ems.

I give up. I switch the light off, climb into bed, and pull the covers over my head.

* * *

The next day's Friday and I slink off to school without a word to anyone. I sit at the back and keep my head down, because I've got a lot of thinking to do. I can tell Si's still annoyed with me, so I give him the day off. He'll catch up with me tonight, but first I've got to work a few things out.

Si needs to learn to trust me.

After school I tell my parents I'm staying at a friend's house overnight, and they're so pleased I even have a friend that they go with it.

Evening arrives and I get something easy to eat and then head off for Bagport's place.

Yeah, I know what you're thinking, and yup, it's weird to just wander in there. But it turns out last night was a bit of a triumph for Mr Big and I'm the bee's knees. You'd've thought that rusty lump of metal with Gubie's head in it would be a disappointment, but Bagport was happy enough with it. Especially since it turns out the cage wasn't tarnished at all, just grubby. It's actually gold-plated.

When I get there, Si's waiting for me, with Ems. Lugubrian's there too, grinding his teeth. I've got a horrible feeling we're a team from here on in.

Great.

'I don't suppose I can talk you out of this?' says Simon.

'Nah. You'll just have to trust me instead.'

'Hah!' barks Lugubrian.

I knock on the metal door behind Bagport's club,

and Ringpull opens it. He grunts, clips me round the ear and then pulls me in. We're going to have a falling out, Ringpull and me, but I let it go for now.

The corner of the storeroom has been cleared, and there's someone there I haven't seen before, a small nervous man with a goatee and no hair. He's got a toolbox open by his feet and on a tripod in front of him is Lugubrian's metal cage. You can really tell it's gold now, and Goatee Man's buffing it up and scraping gunk out of it.

He's not looking too happy, but then Gubie's skull grinning at him while he works might have something to do with that.

'That's a nice paperweight,' I say, and the man looks at me like he doesn't know if I should be there. 'What a lovely hobby.'

Lugubrian's head detaches from his body and circles the man and the box.

'My apparatus!' he says. 'What's he doing to it?'

Really, really weirdly, Goatee Man turns his head like he almost heard something, and looks confused. Then he turns to me and says, 'I'm just cleaning it. Getting it working again. For sale,' he says.

'You can't sell it!' Lugubrian cries. 'It's mine!'

Goatee Man looks around again.

'Did you hear something?'

'Not me,' I say. 'But if your hearing's blocked, ask Dr Ringpull to knock it clear.'

Ringpull raises his hand to box my ears again, so I dart out of the room and straight up the stairs. Goatee Man gives me a dark look as I go.

Bagport's behind his desk, smiling like the white cliffs of Dover, still wearing the horrible shiny suit.

'Hey, there's the kid!' He waves me over. We're best mates now, it seems, though Ringpull's just behind me. 'Chatted to any more rich dead people?'

I shrug. I honestly didn't know that Lugubrian's apparatus was gold, but I'm not complaining.

'You want to go back there tonight, I suppose?' is all I say.

'Well, yeah, I'd love to,' Bagsy chuckles and he gives me a 'haven't you heard?' look. 'There's no way we're doing that now, though, is there?'

I guess I look confused, so he points at the enormous TV screen on the wall opposite his desk and turns the volume up.

Lugubrian's open grave is all over the news. There's a smart young TV journalist in front of a crowd talking to a slightly hysterical woman who lives near the cemetery, then there's a couple of students dressed like vampires who jabber on about the unquiet grave. (Yeah, right! What do they know?) Then after them there's a lurid bio piece about the great Silus Lugubrian and his 'terrible end' which manages to make him sound even freakier than he really is. I'm just staring at it all, because I'm not expecting this. And the thing that's really got everyone going, the hot question on everyone's lips is, 'Where's the skull?'

'You've caused a media storm round Highgate.' says Bagport, 'We'll have to go somewhere else tonight.'

'Me?'

'Don't forget who's in the photos, kid.'

'But...' I don't need to be reminded of those photos. 'But even if we do find more stuff, how can you sell it now? I mean, with all this talk of grave robbing?' I point at the screen. 'The police'll be all over this.'

'What do you mean, "even if"?' Bagport's giving me the murderous eye again. 'Don't forget, kid, you're only interesting as long as you can come up with the goods. There'll be no "even if" if you know what's good for you.'

Simon gives me a meaningful look.

'Who's the beardie downstairs?' I say.

'That's Johnny Sparko,' says Bagsy. 'From the Magic Circle. Up to his slap in debt to me. He'll get that gold cage thing cleaned up and working. And he won't breathe a word.'

'They're saying there's a thousand quid reward for the return of the skull,' I say, waving at the screen.

'Peanuts,' says Bagport. 'There are collectors in this city who'll pay twenty grand plus for a bit of history like that, skull included and no questions asked. This magician geezer caused quite a stir in his day.'

'Looks like he's causing quite a stir now too.'

Bagport glares at me. Maybe we're not such good chums after all. He snaps his fingers and Ringpull almost pulls my arms out of their sockets as he picks me up and dumps me in a chair. Seems I'm supposed to wait like a puppy for its master, but that's okay. I'm already seeing how to get Ems her revenge, and I'm looking forward to helping myself to some too.

After about an hour, Johnny Sparko, the magic guy, comes upstairs and says, 'It's finished'. He's screwing one finger in his ear and looking troubled. I suddenly realize that while Lugubrian's body has been sitting in the seat next to mine, drumming his ghostly fingers, his head has been elsewhere.

There's a wicked SSHNICK as Johnny presses the lever at the side of the apparatus and the twin blades snap together right where your neck would be if you were stupid enough to put it on.

'I got the parts going again, like you said,' says Johnny. 'Oiled them and such like. I changed the spring for a new one and, um, made a few small adjustments to the mechanism that, er, sort of came to me.' And he looks around warily. Just behind him, the ghost head of Silas Lugubrian winks at me.

It feels like the hand of Fate has just reached down and ruffled my hair.

II

A LOAD OF OLD CASSOCKS

It's 10pm before we get moving, and I'm surprised to see that Bagport's actually bringing Lugubrian's device with us. He catches me eyeing it and gives me a slap on the back I could do without.

'It'll be safer in the car,' he says. 'I'm keeping this little prize close while the police are still hunting for it. I'm keeping you and those photos close too, just in case.'

I'm looking for something snarky to say when

Bagport hands me the golden apparatus, just like that. I stare at it, perplexed. Gubie's empty skull grins back. Then *snick* and *snick*, and before you can say 'stuffed', Ringpull's only gone and handcuffed the blasted thing to my wrist!

'Like I said, I'm keeping all my assets close right now,' says Bagport, and Ringpull shoves me in the back to get going. I test the cage for weight. It's heavy.

This was *not* part of the plan!

When we get into the car, Bagsy pours himself a glass of something pink and fizzy while Ringpull gets in with me, complete with camera and pistol. There's another man in the front along with the driver, and I see that all Bagport's scary muscle and gun requirements have been met this evening.

Simon, along with a silent Ems and a grumpy Lugubrian, slips though the closed door and looks worried. I remember then that while Bagport has kind of bought into the whole 'I see dead people' thing, he doesn't actually know I have one who follows me around all the time. Right now, this might be my best chance.

I give Si a secret wink.

He just puffs ectoplasm at me and says nothing.

We drive in silence for a bit and then pull up,

and like the place last night, it's very dark. There's something big nearby, and as I climb from the car I see it's the brooding silhouette of a church, surrounded by bare trees and the standard issue creepy gravestones. There's even a raven cawing somewhere – the whole Gothic shebang. I have no idea where I am, but despite the dark, I see on a board that the church is St Perdita-of-the-Wilderness, and I guess I can look that up later. If there is a later, that is.

As we slip into the graveyard, I haven't forgotten what's expected of me. They're going to want to see some yabbering with spirits and that, and then I'm going to have to come up with a grave to rob, full of gold teeth and silver shoe buckles. The yabbering I can do. Guaranteeing the loot though, that's the tough bit.

'I hope you know what you're doing,' says Si, close by my side.

'S'cool,' I say aloud, and Bagport obviously thinks I'm talking to him.

'You're one creepy kid, you know that?' he says.

'Hey, it's not me who wants to dig up skeletons,' I say, and Ringpull cuffs me round the noggin.

I'm expecting to go on a tour of the graveyard like before, so it's a surprise to find myself round the back of the church, standing next to a dry little wooden door. Bagport's got a torch with some tape over that throws just enough light to see by.

One of Bagport's men steps forward and pushes something into the ancient lock. It looks like a tool, the something does, and I see the man's shoulders struggle for a moment. There's a muffled grinding sound and then a 'pang!' of breaking iron as the man manages to turn the lock with brute force. The door falls open and a couple of bits of twisted metal hit the floor.

I'm shoved inside.

What happens next is one of the weirdest moments I've ever experienced.

Bagport climbs up into the pulpit and leans there, looking like a Las Vegas preacher in his shiny suit, while Ringpull shoves things back off the altar and grunts himself up to sit on it. With a clank, he puts some heavy-duty tools down beside him, though he keeps the camera in his hands. The driver and the lock-breaker pull out guns and stand either side of the small door, which is obviously going to be my only escape route.

'Right, kid,' says Bagport. 'There's no end of posh graves in this place. All you've got to do is do what you did last night, and we can all go home happy. Even you.'

Then they're just waiting there, watching. It's my cue, I guess.

It's gloomy in the church, but my eyes are getting used to it, and there's Bagsy's torch. I take in my surroundings, holding the golden cage in front of me like I'll be selling ice creams at the interval.

The church is obviously very old, and there are inset sculptures and wall-plaques that I know – thanks to History Harris – go back to the Middle Ages. I wonder what made Bagport pick this place. Does he happen to know there's something here? Is this some kind of test? It's a scary moment, especially with the gleam from four pairs of eyes watching me.

'Daniel, look at this,' says Si.

He and the other ghosts are standing beside the tomb of a knight. It's long and low, and the old boy has a small dog by his feet and a sword held in one hand on his chest. Some historic vandal has smashed his face in – people in the past always seemed to be breaking stuff – but you can still see he's wearing a coronet.

I raise my eyebrow at Si.

'If you are planning one of your last-minute surprises,' he says, 'you had better set it in motion now, because there's almost no chance of finding any actual treasure here.'

'I've just got to get them all occupied, that's all,' I whisper. 'This tomb should do it. Thanks, Si.'

'But what *is* your plan?'

'The camera,' I hiss. 'Round Ringpull's neck? If we can distract them with a ghost, maybe I can get it and can take some pics of *them*. Then if I can get out of here, and get it to the police...'

'That is a great many "if"s', Daniel,' says Si.

'Just keep on your toes and get ready to back me up with your party trick, okay?'

'Yes, but I'm bound to say – '

'Speak up, Spirit,' I cry out loud, shouting Si down. 'I can hardly hear you!'

The silence of the men watching me is deafening. Si stares at me for a moment.

'Ah, I see,' he says. 'It's time for the sinister voice, is it? Very well, Master Dyer, I shall see what I can do. But give them a good performance, because I fear this will be the performance of your life.'

Why did he have to add that last bit?

'Come, Spirit, come!' I yell at nothing at all. 'Tell me your troubles!'

I'm glad Mrs C isn't here or she'd make me star

act in the school show, for sure. I lift my arms and point into space and shout 'He comes!', though even I can see there's nothing there. Then I shrink back, holding my arms up like I'm trying to protect myself from some invisible phantom. I stagger and cry out, turn a complete circle and clutch at a pew as I fall to the ground. There's a choirboy's cassock and a pile of bibles on the pew, and they fall down too. Oh, and Gubie's skull in the cage. Let's not forget that.

Eat your heart out, Hamlet!

But if I'm expecting applause, I'm disappointed.

I glance up. Simon's got one hand over his face, but it's the others, the living men, I'm trying to impress. From them there's nothing and I'm wondering if maybe I hammed it up a tad too much.

'How did you know?' I call out to Bagport, but when he replies I can tell from his voice that what he's just seen was a bit too cheesy even for him.

'Know what? This had better not be a wind-up, kid, or you'll wind up falling off the church tower.'

'About the sword?' I say, making stuff up quick. 'The knight's sword? That's why we're here, yeah? You knew it was here in his tomb?' And when there's no reply I add, 'The jewels alone must be worth a fortune.'

There's a long pause.

'You sure about this, boss?' says the lock-breaker.

Bagport looks down from the pulpit, and I can tell even from here that he's suddenly embarrassed. After all the effort he's been to, he'll look pretty stupid if it's all a load of rubbish – which it is – and I'm guessing he'd not want his men seeing that.

'Yeah, I didn't see nuffin, Boss,' goes the driver. 'Is this kid for real?'

'He's a freakin' nutter!' says the lock-breaker and from the altar Ringpull grunts.

Uh-oh.

Bagport looks from his men to me, but it's too dark for me to see his face.

Then he snaps his fingers.

Ringull jumps down off the altar and walks over to me. I'm still lying on the ground, surrounded by bibles and the cassock. I look up at the huge man and wonder if there's even any point getting up, but I don't have to wonder for long because Ringpull leans over and with one hand he pulls me off the ground like I'm the wrong bag of shopping. He reaches his other arm back, and I can tell I'm in for the mother of all head slaps, so I shout 'Wait! The sign!'

'Let him speak,' says Bagport.

71

'Ack…' I manage to choke out past Ringpull's grip. 'Behold the sign! See, where the ghost comes… gah!'

And right beside me the white choirboy cassock lifts off the ground.

It's Simon of course, using his initiative for once, as well as his spooky powers to raise the cassock, but the bad guys don't know that, do they? As it lifts, the cassock fills out and for a moment it takes on the shape of a man.

There are gasps from round the church and Ringpull drops me, wide-eyed. Bagport's swearing again and again in a trembling voice as, in front of four grown and hardened men, the white ghostly figure raises one arm and points at the tomb of the knight.

Then the cassock collapses and I see Si slip out from under it. He's used all his spook powers in one go for that trick, but boy, what a corker! Bagport and his men can't deny the evidence of their own eyes and they're terrified. I think the lock-breaker's actually wet himself.

I stand up and brush myself down.

'Let's get this tomb open then, shall we?' I say.

12

A PEW WITH A VIEW

I push at the stone slab on the tomb, and make a lot of straining noises. This is still part of the act, you understand. I mean, obviously I can't move the slab on my own, but right now I don't actually want to.

'Get back, kid!' gasps Bagport as he staggers down from the pulpit, still swearing, and snapping his fingers like he's close to losing it.

He's genuinely rattled by what he's just seen, but at the same time, the chance to lay his hands on a fabulous jewel-encrusted sword keeps him sane.

'Ringpull, close your gob and get pushing!'

Ringpull pulls himself together and throws his enormous strength against the slab, but it doesn't budge. He tries again and again, and then stops. He pulls his jacket off and rolls up his sleeves. He hangs his jacket on a pew.

Along with the camera.

'Quit gawping!' Bagport yells at the other two men. 'Get your backs into it!' And as the men push their guns into their belts and start shoving, even Mr Big lends a hand. With all four of them straining at the weight there's a short deep scraping sound as the slab begins to move.

'Push harder!' yells Bagsy.

The slab grinds right back, till it's almost toppling onto the ground.

But before that can happen, it's time for me to act.

'Look out, behind you!' I shout, and the men turn to me in alarm.

FLASH!

I get a great shot of the four of them.

FLASH!

Gangsters, grave robbing tools, open tomb – *check*!

74

Then I'm running.

I yank the door open, jump left and race into the dark graveyard, leaving the path behind me.

I don't know which one comes after me first – I was banking on them all being blinded by the flash – but there's someone behind me pretty quick.

'Run, Daniel!' cries Si. 'He's got a gun!'

Crapsticks!

There's a BANG! behind me as the gun goes off and the top of the gravestone I'm ducking behind explodes. Bits of stone hit me in the face, but I can't stop now. I'm zig-zagging and it's dark, so I don't see the person I run into till I've run right smack bang into them.

'Ow!' says a woman's voice. 'What in heaven's name is going on?' And in the dark, as I roll on the ground, I see her standing there. I also see a white square at the woman's neck, as well as the slathering teeth of two enormous dogs at her side.

'Er, hello Vicar,' I say at the top of my voice.

There's a very loud and very rude word in the dark behind me, not the kind of thing lady vicars expect to hear in their own churchyard, I'm sure, but this lady vicar's obviously not the scone and raffle-tickets type. There's an eruption of light as she turns on a torch.

'Get back here this instant!' she roars at the man who was following me, only now he's running away as fast as he can. 'Or I'll set the dogs on you!'

There's more frantic running by the church as four dark figures race down the path, and then there's the sound of car doors slamming. Mr Big's car roars off without its lights on.

Quiet falls over the graveyard.

'Thanks,' I say, as I get to my feet. 'That was, er, more interesting than the last time I went to church.'

There's sudden light as the vicar turns the torch on me. I shield my eyes and try to picture what she must be seeing: a skinny kid with mad hair and purple glasses, and a black leather coat with death's heads Tippexed on it. A kid who's handcuffed to a golden cage with a human skull in it.

She gasps.

What can I say? I mean, somehow I don't expect 'It's not what you think' will quite cover the situation.

I try a grin.

'Look,' I say. 'Let's just pretend I've come to confess.'

* * *

'If you wanted to confess, you should've vandalized the Catholic church up the road,' says Mrs Vicar. 'With me you're just going to need a damned good explanation!'

We're in the vicar's kitchen, and I'm hunched at the table with the cage and skull on my lap, and a dog on either side of me, growling. Well, dogs like bones, don't they? The ghosts of Si, Ems and old Lugubrian are standing behind me, looking guilty too.

Mrs Vicar's a big lady, but I should explain that. I don't mean that she's fat, and she's certainly not butch either. It's just that she's big somehow, like she fills the room, even though she's hardly taller than I am. It's weird. But there's something kind in her face, something that the fury written across it can't quite hide. I'm hoping I'm right about that because I've got some serious talking to do, especially after what she says next.

'I have called the police. They will be here within the hour.'

Crapsticks! But then again...

'Okey dokey,' I say. 'That's only fair. But perhaps I can tell you my story first? I mean, I wouldn't want you thinking I was actually guilty of something.'

Mrs Vicar gives me the gimlet eye. I'm not sure I believe in God, but right here and now I almost do, especially when Mrs Vicar pulls out a newspaper and hands it to me like a judgment from upon high. Lugubrian's open grave at Highgate is still front-page news, then, and yup, they're still looking for the skull.

'Let me guess,' says the vicar. 'This has something to do with you.'

I pat the cage with the skull in it and dial my grin to 'sheepish'.

Then I launch into it, starting with my name. I tell her about Bagport and the kids he forces to work for him, the shoplifting and now the grave robbing, and about the incriminating photos he takes. I explain about Ems, only I call her a friend who got herself killed because of Bagsy, and I explain how I want to avenge her by getting Bagsy caught. Then I get to the bit about how that revenge has gone a tad wrong because the man seems to think I can find treasure in graveyards, and I give her a laugh that's supposed to say, 'What a mad idea!'

Mrs Vicar points at the golden cage.

'How did you know what would be in that magician's grave?'

And here's where I properly lie. I mean, I really don't feel comfortable about giving the 'I see dead people' line in a vicar's kitchen. Behind me I can sense the ghosts cowering back too and probably inspecting their fingernails or staring at their feet. I just shrug and say, 'Luck, I guess.'

There's a pause and the kettle comes to the boil. Despite everything, the vicar is actually making tea.

'So if I'm to believe you, a criminal gang is behind the desecration in Highgate, and now that same gang has just opened the Tomb of Sir Pumphry de Pôville in my very own church, in search of some jewel-encrusted sword that I've certainly never heard about, only somehow you're not to blame despite that grisly object handcuffed to your wrist. Is that really the story you want to tell the police?'

'Yeah.' The grin's probably looking a bit stupid by now, but I stick with it. 'Only, I'd rather not tell the police anything just yet.'

'Oh?' She plonks a mug of black tea down in front of me. She's Good Cop and Bad Cop, all rolled into one.

'Look, see this camera?' I wave it about. 'There's loads of pics on it, but the last two, they're the only ones you need to see. Do you have a computer?'

She nods. I was expecting 'no' as an answer, or if 'yes', then some old clockwork monster from the nineties, but she lifts a pile of newspapers off the table and underneath is a pretty spiffy new-looking laptop.

'Cool,' I say, and I get the card out of the camera and slip it into the side of the machine. She comes round behind me, and the ghosts shrink back and hide in a dark corner. There's just something about this woman.

It takes me a moment, but then the pics I took are up. You can see Bagport and his cronies clear as day, and behind them the open tomb. Ringpull is actually holding a crowbar. It couldn't be better.

Mrs Vicar reaches past me, and before I can stop her she taps the back arrow a few times. The picture changes to one of me down in Gubie's dug-out grave, holding a spade. I look round at her from the corner of my eye, and to find she's staring right into me.

I swallow.

'Right, I've seen enough,' she says. 'Now you listen to me, young man, and I'll tell you exactly what I'm going to do with you.'

13

TEA, BUT NO SYMPATHY

'You're what?' I say, too stunned to believe my ears.

'You heard,' says Mrs Vicar. 'I'm letting you go.'

'Cool!'

'But only because I know you're going to be caught anyway.'

Not so cool.

'Which is why,' she goes on, 'you are going to hand yourself in. If the police find you here, they'll throw the book at you. But if you go to them and turn yourself in, it will stand in your favour.'

The grin finally falls off my face and curls up to die somewhere between my feet.

'Oh, don't look so glum,' says Mrs Vicar. 'If what you have told me is true, the police will have all the evidence they need on the camera's memory card. Someone like this Carl Bagport will already be known to them.'

'Yeah, but there's also – '

Mrs Vicar reaches past me again and starts tapping the keyboard. In a moment she's deleted all but the last two photos from the memory card. Though not, I see, from her hard drive. Then she ejects the card and sticks it back into the camera.

'I'll say I found this when I disturbed the intruders. When you hand yourself in, you can say the camera is yours.'

The grin leaps back up and starts dancing under my nose.

'But why…?'

'Why am I doing this? Because whatever part you have played in disturbing the dead, spending the night with that skull, in contemplation of your sins, will tell you once and for all if you are guilty or not.'

And she's pointing one horrified finger at Gubie's apparatus. 'The rest is unimportant.'

There's the sound of a car outside, and headlights flash across the kitchen window. The police! I'm on my feet in a shot, but already I can tell there's no safe way out the front.

'You can leave by the back door,' says Mrs Vicar. 'Here's the number of a taxi firm, and here's a twenty-pound note. The next time I see your face I expect it will be in the local paper, explaining this sorry business and donating the reward for the return of the skull to charity. Otherwise I'll just happen to find some more photos that I'm sure the police would like to see. Understand?'

I nod, and head to the back of the kitchen and freedom, even as the front doorbell rings. The three ghosts slink along behind me. I guess none of us can get out of there fast enough. Still, I turn in the door before I close it, to say thanks, but the vicar beats me to it.

'May you find peace,' she says.

I'm about to reply when I notice she's not looking at me at all, but *past* me. I glance behind and see no one there but the three ghosts. Then a chill slides down my spine.

Is she looking at *them*?

'You mean you can…?' I say, turning back, but Mrs Vicar is gone. I hear the distant sound of the front door opening.

'Daniel, let us be gone from this place!' comes the voice of Simon, and I don't need telling twice. I pull the door shut and run silently across the vicar's moonlit garden.

14

IN WHICH WE ALL GO DOWN

After a night like that, even the fact that it's the weekend doesn't make the dawn any easier. All I can think about is the handcuffs and how they itch, and how I'd just love to chuck Lugubrian's stupid apparatus in the Thames, skull and all. At least his ghost has drifted off. When the Saturday morning sun finally rises, it's just me and Si and Ems, sitting in my room, staring at the telly and hardly daring to speak.

And all I can think about is what's going to happen to me when I give myself up, because somehow *not* doing what Mrs Vicar says just doesn't seem like an option, especially since if they do arrest Bagport, he's hardly going to be quiet about my name, now, is he? First, though, we're waiting for the news to come on, and I'm eating stale tortilla chips as the clock ticks round.

It's a long time before there's anything about the open tomb at the church. Then…

'Police have confirmed that arrests have been made in connection with the Highgate incident, following a similar raid on a church last night…'

And we're all staring at the screen as Bagport's driver from the night before, as well as the man who broke the lock, are seen struggling as they're shoved into a police van outside Bagport's club. I give out a whoop of relief. Just a small one, mind, but still.

'There you are, Emeline!' says Simon, brightening with me. 'At least it looks like we have brought you the vengeance you wanted. Are you satisfied?'

'Hmm,' says Ems. 'I don't see Bagport there.'

It's true. Mr Big himself has not been shown being arrested, and then…

'According to a police spokesman, a number of people are still being sought in this bizarre affair.'

I sigh. There's no getting away from it – the bizarre bit's mostly me. And it sounds like Bagsy's yet to be bagged.

'If Bagport's still out there, Ems,' I say, 'I can at least tell an ugly tale about him when they arrest me. His network of kids is over in any case.'

'And they will find the pictures of you, Emeline,' says Si. 'On his computator. The reason behind your death will come out and your parents will know that you were forced to lift from shops.'

Ems looks up and there's almost a smile. This is part of what she's wanted all along, after all. But the smile doesn't last long.

'Stop trying to get out of it,' she snaps at us. 'You said you'd bring him down, and until I see Bagport crawling in front of a judge, you two owe me a result.'

'Truly,' admits Si. They're both looking at me. I nod slowly. I know what they're thinking. I look at my watch and see that it's nearly midday. High noon. Time to hand myself in.

I'm still dressed as I was the night before – well, I can hardly get changed with a skull chained to my wrist, can I? – so I get up and wrap Gubie's apparatus

87

in a plastic bag. I slip downstairs while my parents are watching the telly, shout a quick goodbye that they don't get up for, and head down to the local cop shop. Looks like Dan Dyer's about to go out of business for a bit. There isn't even time for a closing down sale.

'Will you wait for me?' I ask Si, with a lump in my throat. 'I mean, when they let me out, will I have to look for a new sidekick?'

'Don't be a nincompoop, Daniel,' sniffs Si. 'I waited two hundred and fifty years for you, I can wait a few more.'

'Eh? What do you mean by that?'

Si looks a bit flustered.

'I misspoke,' he said. 'All I meant was that I would wait.'

'Oi, cut out the luvvie duvvies, you pair of muppets!' says Ems. 'You're not old enough to go to prison, dipstick, they'll probably just give you a hard time with questions. Maybe an ASBO for your mantelpiece. You can put all the blame on Bagport, no problem. I mean, you're hardly going to chain *yourself* to a dead magician's skull are you?'

'Well, no,' I say. She's right.

'So pull your tights up and be a man, you numpty!'

You know, despite everything, I'm going to miss Ems.

I'm just about to say something cheery and brave when all the wind is knocked out of my lungs. Something big lifts me off the ground, and as I try to focus on what it might be, something else that looks a lot like a fist knocks me senseless.

* * *

When the world clears again, and the pain in my head finally gets my full attention, I find myself looking at someone I'd hoped I wouldn't have to see again up close.

'Well, well, the kid who sees dead people,' says Bagport, through his teeth.

We're in the back of his car, and even with my head reeling, I can tell that like me, Bagport has spent the night in his clothes. No one can have two suits that shiny. In fact, I guess he's spent the night in his car too, now his club's been raided. But he's obviously been back to his lair because there's a pile of computer equipment, keyboards and mobile phones in the back with us. In fact, all the stuff the police would need to make a proper conviction stick.

'Get a move on, Ringpull!' calls Bagport to the front seat, and I turn to see the thick neck of Mr Big's hard man as he grinds through the gears. Gold fluffy dice swing from the rear view mirror. We're in the white stretched limo, which the police must be looking for, so I guess that explains the nervous twitch in Bagport's face.

'Daniel?' Si's caught us up and he's in the car, with Ems too. 'Have they hurt you?'

I shake my head, which Bagsy sees and thinks it's his cue to come in with some cheesy lines.

'You screwed up my life, kid, so I'll screw up yours. You may think those photos will be the end of me, but I'll make sure of your end first. Ha!'

'Yeah, well, I'll tell the police everything,' I manage to say. 'I'll tell them what you did to Ems. Who do you think they'll listen to, a kid like me or a scumbag like you? You're going down, mate.'

Bagport leans forward and grinds his index finger into my chest, one eye squinting and the other wide open.

'Maybe, maybe, maybe.' His voice is wild and freaky. 'But you're going down further, much further. Right down to the bottom where the fishes fart. *Mate*! Ha, ha!'

He's pretty hysterical, but I don't like the sound of this. I make a grab for the door handle but he kicks out at me. His crocodile-skin boot makes contact with my chin, and that's the last thing I remember for Death knows how long.

15

THE GHOST OF A CHANCE

The next thing I know it's getting dark, and I've obviously been out for a few hours. There's a bumping, splashing sound, and I'm guessing that's what woke me up, but I can't think about that now because I realize my hands are tied. Tightly.

Behind my back.

I roll over and catch my chin on a computer monitor. I'm still in the back of Bagport's car, only now I'm on my own, surrounded by all that electronic stuff from Bagsy's office. Sitting up, I see that the car's parked at a steep angle, on a slope running down. Above me are what look like huge dockside containers and a crane. Something is slapping at the back of the car, and I strain to get my head up to look. Then I say something rude, because what's behind me is the sea!

And it's lapping right round the back of the car.

'Daniel! Can you hear me?' yells Si's voice.

I twist around again, and see him wringing his hands. Ems is there too.

'We thought you were dead,' she says. 'Well, I did, but Frilly Knickers here said he'd know if you were.'

'Where are we?' I manage to say, and I yank at the knots round my wrists. 'Is that really the sea?'

Simon nods, his eyes wide.

'Si, please tell me the tide's going out.'

'We're at the port of Harwich,' says Si. 'The back end of it. That scoundrel Bagport is planning to catch a boat to Holland, I overheard him saying so.'

'I don't care where Mr Fake Tan and Chinos goes on holiday!' I'm yelling myself now. 'The tide, Si?'

'Alas, it rises.'

'Dan, you have to get free!' cries Ems. 'The water's already coming into the car.'

Since when has she called me Dan? It's normally 'turnip brain' or 'pinhead' or something. Now I know I should be worried, especially when I look again at all the stuff crammed into the back seat. It's just about everything that Bagsy needs to get rid of if he wants to escape a long time in clink. And that includes your favorite psychic detective.

'He's going to let me drown, isn't he?' I ask the two ghosts, though it's a stupid question. Of course he is.

'I shouldn't have got you involved!' Ems is really upset. 'I always knew he was too dangerous.'

'Relax,' I say, though I'm near to panic myself. My arms are completely fixed behind me, and already there's a trickle of water around the back door. 'Simon can use his spook powers to loosen the knots, can't you, Si? Si?'

'Daniel, I have been trying. But after elevating the cassock in the church last night… well, the knot is fiendishly tight and I fear my powers are insufficiently recuperated. Daniel, you must get free by yourself. And quickly! Zooks, see how the waters rise!'

I tug at the ropes till my wrists almost bleed, but there's no way I can loosen the knots. There's a little give, but I can't get my hands through. I turn and look about wildly. Is there something I can break to make a sharp edge? Can I cut the rope?

No.

'Daniel, think! Is there something from one of our previous clients you can use?'

I rack my brains. I've picked up a lot over the years, and you'd be amazed at what I can do, but escaping from the back of cars isn't a skill I've needed before.

Escape…

'I can drive the car…' I gasp out. 'I got that last year, remember? Si, could you start the car?'

'Maybe, but with your hands tied…'

'I don't know how I can get them free, Si. I just don't know.'

There's a sudden upturn in the pressure of the water spraying round the doors and into the back seat. I stare ahead up the steep slope, and in the gloom I see two figures standing at the top, watching. They have a small car behind them, and I can tell it's Bagport and Ringpull, smoking and waiting to see me go under. The waterline is already washing over the rear windows. I've got about five minutes, max.

'There must be someone who can help you escape!' I'm touched that Ems is so worried about me, but there's that word again, 'escape', and there's no getting away from the idea that comes into my head. A truly horrible idea. And yet...

I look at Si, and something in his wild eyes suggests he's thinking it too.

'Daniel, I could get him very quickly. He could be here in a minute or two, and I'm certain he can help. He was a noted escapologist in his day.'

I tug at the ropes again. There's got to be some other way.

'Just give me a moment to think…'

'You don't have many moments left,' says Si. 'Let me fetch him!'

I struggle again, but slump forward into the computers in defeat. The water is already creeping up my ankles and the icy spray from around the door is soaking the rest of me. I have no choice. It's the North Sea, or…

'Okay, Si. Get him.'

Then Si's gone. Ems is swirling around in front of me, flapping.

'What's he doing? Who has he gone to get?'

'S'okay, Ems,' I say. She's still my client after all. 'There's someone who can help me out of this. I'm going to have to do a deal, that's all. It's just that the price is going to be, er, high.'

'What do you mean? What deal? What price?'

The water hits my thigh and it's freezing. My legs are already going numb. The car makes a groan as it begins to shift in the tidal water.

'The ultimate price,' I say and shake the golden cage that's still chained to my wrist. But Ems looks blank.

'I don't understand,' she says.

'But I do,' says a gravelly voice. 'So, you're finally ready to do a deal with your old pal Silas are you? Need a little touch of magic, eh?' And the sallow face of Silas Lugubrian, Gentleman of Miracles, leers down at me in the gloom, as the water creeps towards my belly button.

All I can do is nod.

16

A TOUCH OF THE HOUDINIS

'You must swear it.' Silas Lugubrian looks right into my eyes. 'You must swear to perform my trick in public.'

'I'm o-only looking for a d-down payment…' I stutter. The cold is getting right into the heart of me.

'It doesn't matter what you call it,' says Lugubrian, 'I know how you work, boy, I know the deal. I give you a little of myself – in this case my escapology skills – and you do what I ask. I'm happy to pay you in advance, but what guarantee can you give *me*, eh?'

The water's creeping up my middle. If he doesn't hurry my hands will be too numb to manipulate the knots anyway.

'Just do it!' Si shouts at Gubie. 'He has but moments!'

'I p-promise,' I manage to say. 'G-get me out of here, and I'll t-take on your case.'

Lugubrian gives a ghostly huff and looks uncertain. But he's got me, he can see that. If I go against my promise, my reputation amongst the desperate dead will be ruined, and I just know the old magician will haunt me for the rest of my life. He can probably see all this in my eyes, and he smiles, his teeth spreading before me like yellow tombstones.

'Very well,' croons the ghost of Silas Lugubrian, 'Are you ready?'

I nod, trembling.

Gubie's head advances towards mine. It gets closer and closer until it dissolves and passes through my eyes like smoke. There's a rush of cold to my brain, colder even than the seawater chill that's gripping my body – so cold that it feels like icicles have formed inside my skull – and I cry out.

Then as soon as it's started, it's over. Gubie's spirit passes out through my ears in streams of ectoplasm and his head reforms. In my skull the cold melts away.

But not entirely.

Somewhere in my memory I sense an unfamiliar little packet of experience that wasn't there before, experience that is not my own.

This is how they all pay me – a tiny portion of their life, gifted to me in return for my services. It's a little piece of the dead that will live on in me once they have passed on to the Hereafter. And in this case, it's everything Lugubrian knows about escapology.

But this is no time for chat.

My fingers are already reaching into the knots, doing things they've never done before with the practiced ease of someone else's skill. And it turns out Silas Lugubrian, Gentleman of Miracles, was really quite good at the old Houdini business, because the knot's already starting to slip, even as the water reaches my shoulders.

'Si,' I shout, 'start the freakin' engine!'

Simon shoves his hand into the car's ignition – he's started cars for me before – but nothing happens for a moment, and I remember he's still running on empty. Then, just as I throw the ropes away from my hands and grab the front seats, there's a gasp from Si and a reluctant rumble as the engine coughs into life. I drag myself tumbling into the front seat. I seize the steering wheel, ram the gear stick into first, and jab my foot down on the submerged accelerator. The engine screams.

'Advance!' cries Si.

'I'm trying!' I shout, as I let out the hand brake to relieve the engine's roar. The car eases up the slope, painfully slowly. I'm lucky the engine wasn't under water yet, but the exhaust is, and the back of the car's full of the North Sea too and probably weighs more than a boatload of overweight Vikings. There's a riot of bubbles in the water behind me, but the car still only inches forward.

'Faster!' shouts Ems, as if I need telling.

Like a reluctant sea monster, Bagsy's naff stretched limo emerges from the waves, rising up the slope at about two miles an hour, seawater pouring out in great torrents, the whole chassis juddering.

The radio comes on. It's Justin Bieber.

'Cool,' says Ems.

I say something my mother would be ashamed of as I switch on the headlights, full beam.

Up ahead, Bagport and Ringpull are staring down at me in astonishment, raising their arms against the sudden dazzle. But that's not all they're raising. In a moment they've both reached into their coats and pulled out pistols. I duck as the first bullet punches through the windscreen, showering me with small cubes of glass.

'They are firing at us!' yells Si.

'Yeah, I know!' I shout back, as another bullet explodes a computer monitor on the seat behind me. 'Shut up and let me drive!'

The car begins to pick up speed, and the men up front empty their weapons in a burst of sustained gunfire, causing the car to judder with impacts. My head's right down, but my foot is too, and now we're rushing up the slope like a lifeboat going the wrong way. There's an almighty CRASH as we smack into the small car at the top of the slope, shoving it to one side. With the engine screaming at me to change gear, we shoot out onto the dockside, and I sit up just in time to steer us away from a crane. There's one last shot fired from behind and the fluffy dice vanish in a puff of gold polyester.

I let out a laugh of triumph, slip her into fourth, and race away into the night.

17

BULLETS, BUMPERS AND BLUE FLASHING LIGHTS

It's not quite time to celebrate though. As I rush past astonished dock workers and hurl the limo between lorries and into the traffic beyond, I spot two headlights swerving into the road behind me. Somehow I just know it's Bagport and Ringpull, and I realise they'll be so desperate to catch me that there'll be no more fancy stuff with ropes. I'm driving for my life.

'Where're we going?' asks the ghost of Ems.

'I think it's time to do what Mrs Vicar said,' I get out through gritted teeth, as we narrowly overtake an elderly driver in a hat. 'We've got to go to the police.'

'Do you think you can convince them of Bagport's guilt?' says Si.

'Are you kidding me? With all this computer stuff in the car, we're carrying enough to get Bagport banged up for years. No wonder he's not even bothering to catch that ferry to Holland. He'll have nowhere to run if we can get all this to the cops.'

I glance into the remains of the rear-view mirror, and see that the car pursuing me has gained and is just a few vehicles back, swerving as it looks for a way through the traffic.

'But he won't let you go,' says Ems, looking back too. 'You don't know what he's like. He'll kill you, run you off the road.'

As if to emphasise this, there's a shot and a bullet slams into the back of the car.

'You must perform my trick before then,' says Lugubrian, whose body is sitting in the back with its arms folded while his head rolls around on the dash. 'You are no good to me dead, boy. Let him kill you afterwards.'

'If you can't say anything helpful, just can it!' I shout. 'I'm not letting him get me, okay?'

But the truth is, it's not looking good and I haven't got a clue where I'm going. I can drive, thanks to a payment from an old client, but that payment didn't come with sat nav, did it? I'm racing on blind. All I can do is keep following signs for London and hope the police pull Bagsy over for insane driving whilst in charge of a gun or something.

I press the accelerator down, even though it sounds like a bullet has got into the engine.

We drive on and on, and it seems like ages before the lights of the London suburbs are flashing past. But by now I'm daring to hope again because, finally, the traffic police have cottoned on to the desperate race I'm running. There are sirens now, and I can see blue lights behind us, but every time I slow down, Bagport gains on us and takes another potshot. All I can do is hurtle on and hope some more.

Suddenly, on a road sign, I spot somewhere I know – a place near where I live – and I skid sharply into the exit, bouncing off a crash barrier with a torrent of sparks. Bagport's taken by surprise by this and almost misses the exit.

Almost.

At the last minute he swerves and jumps the barrier – actually jumps it! – and crashes down on the road right behind us.

'Crapsticks!'

By now there's a crowd of blue lights behind us. Why don't they drive faster?

I mount the pavement and break through a painted fence, storming into a car park. Yeah, I know that sounds nuts, but I'm starting to recognize the streets and I know I can get through here, and by now all I can think of is getting home. Bagport's right behind me, but his car takes a hammering from the wooden debris that flies round the limo. Both our cars must look a right state as we bounce over the pavement into the street beyond.

'Daniel, why is there a red lamp twinkling?' says Si in his old-fashioned way, and he points at the dashboard. I haven't once looked at the fuel gauge, but I'm staring at it now. It's right down on empty.

'Oh, frack, we're almost out of petrol!'

'The tank's been hit,' says Ems, pocking her head out the window. 'There's been petrol pouring out the back for ages.'

'What! Why didn't you tell me?'

'I thought it was seawater. Don't shout at me.'

'This is mad!' I shout anyway, and it is. We're only five minutes away from home and Mum and Dad and whatever protection I'll find there until the police breeze up, but now I seriously doubt we'll get even that far.

Just then, Bagport's car catches up and I see both him and Ringpull. Their eyes dance with furious delight as they get abreast of us, and then they slam into our side.

The limo swerves, and I fight to correct it, but I'm on the other side of the road now and there's a lorry.

'Hold on!' I shout, even though there's really no need for ghosts to hold on, is there? I turn the wheel hard into the pavement and run the limo straight into a shoe shop, ducking down as the window glass sprays through the car. I look up and get smacked in the gob by a boot, but in the mirror I spot a whole display's worth of ladies' shoes pile through Bagsy's windscreen, stiletto heels and all.

'A creditable hit!' cries Si, as Bagsy's car appears to lose control.

But I've got no time to cheer along. I fight with the wheel again and bring the limo into a straight line, and thank Death there's a second shop window at the back, facing onto the next street. With a crash like a thunderclap, we erupt through it and back out into the night.

I skid round onto the road, and the engine gives a cough. The tank must be nearly dry.

I look behind and I can hear sirens everywhere, even the thrum-thrum of a helicopter, but there's no police to be seen. As I watch, I see Bagport's car trundle out of the ruin of the shoe shop and turn into the road behind us.

But I've noticed something else. We're not going to make it home, that's for sure, but I know the street we're in really well. It's a street I see five days a week, because at the end of it is my school.

And tonight's the night of the school show, remember? Crowds. I'll be safe there until the police catch us up.

I press the accelerator to the floor, but even as we surge forward there's a falling off of power and the engine coughs again.

'Come on!'

I jab my foot up and down, and I see the entrance to my school up ahead, but just then Bagport and Ringpull get abreast of me again, and Bagport points his pistol.

How much freakin' ammo have they got?!

I set the wheel for the school gate – there's no time to turn into it properly – and drop below the dashboard. Bagsy fires two shots. The front tire explodes and we go into a spin. I brace myself and shout 'Crapsticks!' as we pile smack bang into the brick gateposts of my school with a sound like the end of the world.

18

GUBIE GETS HIS WAY

When I sit up, my head is ringing. There's light dancing around me and smoke and heat.

'Daniel!' says Si. 'Daniel, get out! The car is ablaze.'

It's true. But with petrol pouring through the back of the car all that time, this shouldn't be suprising. I shake the confusion out of my head, reset my purple specs, and try the door.

Locked.

I shuffle over to the passenger seat and the buckled door falls open, tumbling me out onto the tarmac of the school car park. I look about as I lie on the ground and see Bagport's small car has smashed into the chain link fence, and wedged tightly, half way through. As I watch, I see movement in the front seat and Bagsy's door opens.

'Gargh!' he shouts, and before I can get to my feet, he raises his pistol at me and pulls the trigger.

Click!

'Get up and run!' Ems and Si shout exactly the same thing and I don't need to be told twice. I'm on my feet, clutching Gubie's apparatus with his skull rattling around inside, and I stagger to the school. Behind me police cars are screeching up to the school gate, but the limo, which is blazing furiously as the computers catch alight, is wedged between the gateposts and blocking the way.

So much for all that evidence.

I stumble up to the school door and heave it open. The lights are on. The door to the assembly hall is at the far end and I see it's packed for the school show, and hear the tortured wail of a lone violin from within.

Standing in front of the door is the leering ghost of Silas Lugubrian.

'You were never really going to avoid this moment, you do realize that, don't you, boy?'

The violin misses a high note, and makes a sound like scraping ribcages.

'That's what I like most about you, Gubie,' I say, running towards him, clutching his apparatus. 'Your cheery, smiley ways.'

He steps to one side and bows to the door.

'Enter! Your destiny and my fortune await!'

'Nah,' I say, as at the last minute I swerve to a door on the left, just as Bagport and Ringpull burst into the corridor behind me. Well, you don't think I'm actually going to do his stupid magic trick, do you?

'No!' shouts Lugubrian. 'Curse you, boy, if you go against your word! Curse you!'

'Relax,' I shout behind me as I push into the dark room beyond the door. 'I said I'd take on your case, and I will.' I'm just going to find some other way to show off his trick without actually putting my own head in it, that's all.

But there's no time for this now, I've got to hide until the police can get Bagport.

I skid to a halt at the end of the room, which is full of sports equipment, and swing behind a cupboard. Ems and Si swoop into the room and join me.

The door bursts open and the light goes on. I glance round and see Bagport, his golden hair wild and his shiny suit crumpled. He looks like a boil-in-the-bag Turkey Twizzler. Beside him the low brow of Ringpull turns here and there, searching.

Why aren't the police here yet?

'Get out here, kid!' shrieks Bagport. They both snatch up cricket bats from a box beside them. With the police surrounding the building it looks like all they have to look forward to now is smashing me into a pulp while they still can.

I go really still, but something a bit odd happens. Gubie's skull shifts in the cage, making a rattling sound, and Bagsy hears it. You'd almost think the magician did it deliberately.

'Aaargh!' Bagport bellows as he runs at me, cricket bat raised. I shoot out of my hiding place just as the bat thwacks against the cupboard, and I run. I try to get back out the door I came in, but Ringpull throws himself across it.

'This way!' calls Si, pointing to a second door at the back of the room. I know that this door leads to the backstage area of the school hall, but I can't be choosy any more. I fling a handful of plastic sports-day hoops at Ringpull, duck under Bagsy's bat as it slices through the air, and throw myself at the door.

I burst through into the dark behind the stage. I trip on something, and stumble forward, my legs running in emergency mode as I try to stop. By the time I realize where I am, I'm standing in a spotlight, right slap bang in the middle of the stage.

Also in the spotlight is a girl with a ponytail I vaguely recognize. She's holding a violin at her throat and staring at me, her mouth wide open. Beyond her I can see hundreds of faces in the dark behind the spotlight, though I can only see a few of them clearly. Down at the front, a look of scandalized disbelief on his face, is History Harris, and near him Mrs C is staring at me with a shocked but expectant look. The theatrical light probably looks lovely as it glints off the golden cage in my hands, highlighting the empty sockets of the dead man's skull inside.

So there I am, on stage.

Despite everything I ever said, I'm appearing at the school show. And everyone's watching.

The ghost of Silas Lugubrian appears at my side.

It's just so not fair!

19

CURTAINS

The silence is so intense you can hear Mrs C's lipstick crack as she smiles encouragement at me.

No one in the hall knows what's going on outside. I can feel the eyes of everyone there shift from me to the golden cage in my hands, and back to me again.

They all read the papers, watch the telly – they must know what it is I'm holding. They know about the spring-loaded blades on Gubie's apparatus and about what happened to the Gentleman of Miracles one snowy London night in 1882.

They must all be wondering if I'm mad enough.

Just then Bagport and Ringpull burst onto the stage, and are so surprised to find themselves there that they skid to a halt too, just beyond the spotlight. I glance past them and see uniforms scrabbling into the wings, but even the police seem reluctant to break the spell.

And you know, I can't help thinking that Gubie's right. It really is like the Fates have conspired to get me here, on stage, with his wretched magic trick in my hands. As I look down at the audience and hear the way it holds its collective breath, I've half a mind to put the blasted thing on, chop my head off and just have done with it. I even hold the apparatus up in the light.

As if on cue, my hand catches the mechanism, and the skull falls out. It lands right at my feet and grins up at me.

There's a smattering of automatic applause.

Beside me in the circle of light Silas Lugubrian strikes a dramatic pose. He's standing before the audience as if they can see him.

'Ladies and gentlemen,' he declares, even though no one can hear him except me. 'I give you the amazing, the stupefying, Lugubrian's Head-in-his-hands Illusion!' And he bows.

'I…' I begin, looking up at the golden cage which I'm now holding above my head, seeing that the two steel blades are primed to snap shut either side of my neck. 'I perform this magic trick in the name of… of…'

But do you know what?

Cobblers to it!

I mean, what am I, a puppet of Dame Fortune or something? Don't *I* get a say?

I give the skull at my feet an almighty kick, sending it sailing into the dark above the audience, and I turn to leg it off the other side of the stage. This is one head that's going to stay on its shoulders.

There's screaming chaos in the hall, and I'm wishing this nightmare would just come to an end, but before I can get off the other side of the stage two enormous hands grab me.

It's Ringpull.

Before I can even react he's dragged me back centre stage and plonked me down in a chair, directly in the spotlight, my hands clasped behind my back in one of his. The police jump forward, from both sides of the stage, but before they can get there Bagport grabs the golden cage and rams it down over my head.

Suddenly I'm staring out between the bars, the edges of the blades scraping my neck as I struggle.

So I don't struggle.

'Get back!' shouts Bagport, his clumsy great fingers grabbing the hair-trigger release mechanism of the twin blades. The edges tremble and I go very, very still.

The police skid to a halt. As I thought, everyone knows what Lugubrian's apparatus is capable of.

'Now now, sir. This isn't the way...' says a copper, who tries to edge a little closer.

'Get *BACK*!' shrieks Bagport. 'Or the kid gets his first shave!'

The police edge away again. Silence falls once more, and everyone is watching. The spotlight has never felt hotter.

'Daniel...' says Si, and I can see him and Ems standing down in the audience, but there's nothing Si can do to help me now, and nothing he can say. The only one who isn't frozen to the spot is Silas Lugubrian.

'No no, *no!*' he cries. 'This isn't how it goes. I introduce the trick, you flourish it around, *then* you press the lever. How can I work in such conditions?'

'I want a clear path out of here,' calls Bagport to the police. 'I'm bringing the kid with me. If anyone even comes near... *SSHNICK*! Comprendez?'

Lugubrian strides up to Bagport.

'You are ruining everything! The adjustments have been made. Let the boy operate the apparatus!'

But of course, no one can see or hear him.

'All right, sir,' says the policeman to Bagport. 'We'll clear the stage. Just go nice and easy now.' And with that the police edge back further still. The girl with the violin finally realizes that her act is over and flounces off in a huff. Mr Big is back in control.

And I've just about had it up to, well, up to where Gubie's blades will meet in my windpipe if Bagport presses that lever. Why is it always him who calls the shots? Why am I the doormat every time? The blades dig further into my neck.

But then I remember that adjustments *were* made to the mechanism, and that old Silas Lugubrian *was* a noted stage magician. This deathtrap apparatus over my head is a *trick*, after all. So what if...?

'Ladies and gentlemen,' I declare in a voice even Gubie would be proud of. Everyone goggles back.

'Shut up!' snarls Bagport.

'...I give you the amazing, the stupefying, Lugubrian's Head-in-his-hands Illusion!'

And before anyone can say or do anything more I reach up and press the lever. The steel blades spring together.

SSHNICK!

20

THE END OF IT ALL

My head falls forward and there's blood everywhere.

For a moment I can actually feel the blades.

Then I raise my head again and grin up at Bagport, because the 'Head-in-his-hands' Illusion only freakin' well works, doesn't it? It works!

The blood? Oh yeah, that's not me. Bagport got his little finger in the way, didn't he? And if you look carefully you can see it, rolling off the stage.

There's a sudden mixture of screaming and confused applause from the hall, and I stand up – Ringpull is too astonished to remember to hold me down – and take a bow.

I hear Bagport start screaming himself, but just then the police snap out of it and pile into the stage like a rugby match, wrestling the bad guys to the ground. One policeman comes at me, but I hold up the wrist that's handcuffed to the golden cage and he pauses. Then he nods, puts his hand on my shoulder, and speaks out in a clear voice.

'All right, son. We'll have you out of there in a jiffy.'

Incredibly, the audience takes this as if it's the end of the act and the crowd goes wild.

Amongst the cheering I can hear Bagport's manic, freaked-out voice shouting from beneath two policemen.

'No proof! No proof! It's the kid… he cut off my finger! I've done nothing wrong!'

'Sergeant,' I say to a policeman in a flak jacket who might be nothing of the sort, but so what. 'Officer, this man has been blackmailing kids to shoplift for him, resulting in the death of a girl called Emeline Parker. He's also into a ton of other dodgy stuff, but you can find all the evidence you need on his hard drive.'

'If you mean the computers in the back of the burning limo,' says the copper, 'I doubt we'll get much off them now, but at least...'

''S'okay, I got copies,' I interrupt. 'Shiny suit, top pocket,' and I nod at Bagsy. A policeman reaches his fingers into the pocket and fishes out the USB stick that Mr Big so thoughtfully tucked in there the first night he had me in his car.

'NO!' Bagport's really yelling now. 'When I get my hands on you, kid, I'll...'

But I don't hear the rest because Carl Bagport's being dragged away to face the music. And I don't mean Justin Bieber.

Then someone somewhere remembers that this is a theatre, and the curtains creak in to a close. I catch a last glimpse of the wild, cheering, disbelieving, frenzied audience. Just as the curtains are about to meet in the middle, I see the crooked black shape of Silas Lugubrian standing in the spot-lit gap, one hand fixed as ever in the small of his back, the other flourishing as he bows to his applauding public.

Looks like he got what he wanted after all.

By the time the curtains have closed, he's gone.

The police don't know what to do with me straight away. They find me a female police constable to sit next to in the wings, while someone tries to locate my parents. As if they'd have gone to the school show anyway, even if they'd known I'd be popping up on stage.

The lady copper bustles up to make a fuss, but after taking in the death's head coat, the china false eye round my neck and the bloody golden cage that's hanging from my wrist, she backs away, mumbling something about making tea.

So then I'm just left sitting there on my own, in the dark. As ever.

Of course, that's not strictly true, is it? I'm never completely alone. Simon's there, looking so relieved that there's almost a touch of colour in his cadaverous cheeks. He's muttering 'Zooks!' and 'Zounds, Daniel!' a lot but I just shrug and grin like it's all cool, even though my left leg is still trembling.

'You were amazing!' says a voice.

I turn to see who spoke and I see the ghost of Ems there. She's looking at me with such soft round eyes that I almost wish she'd call me 'numpty' and shout like she usually does. At least then I'd be on the same old ground I'm always on with the opposite sex. But it looks a lot like adoration that's shining out of those big spooky eyes, and adoration for me at that. Hey, a girl likes me!

Trust me to have a ghost girlfriend.

'Hi, Ems.'

'You took control of the whole situation! You were so brave to press the lever yourself, but you must have known all along it would work, didn't you? Though I can't see how. You're amazing!'

I glance at Si and he glances back. I knew nothing of the sort, but it's not every day a girl looks at me like this, so I just shrug again.

'All in a night's work.'

'You got him for me – Bagport, I mean. I'm so happy!'

'I'm glad for you, Ems. I hope you can rest in peace now, like Mrs Vicar said.'

'But there is one thing left to do, isn't there?'

I groan inside. What does she want now? But then I see she's coming closer and closer…

'Your payment, Dan.'

I'm about to mumble something about offering her a discount for all the palaver when her lips reach mine.

Now, imagine you've got a butterfly, yeah? And you make it really, really cold? Now imagine it brushes its wing across your mouth, only it's not really there, at all, the wing, it's more of an idea butterfly? Yeah? Only, it's so delicate it turns your heart upside down, and…

Ah, forget it. Ems is kissing me. And it's… wow!

I open my eyes and I can hardly see her. The air around me feels like a crisp frosty morning with a winter sun, on Christmas Day in the snow.

And then she's gone.

Once again it's just me and Si.

'Daniel?'

'S'okay, Si.'

He puts his hand on my shoulder. I can't actually feel it, but right now it's nice to know it's there.

'The shoplifting skills?' he asks.

And I grin.

'Yeah, she knew I wanted those all along.'

I rummage my mind and feel Ems's gift to me nestling there, not far from the blob of escapology experience I got from Gubie. Ems has gone on to the Hereafter, but a tiny part of her will live on in me. And you never know when a little pick-pocketry will come in handy, not with my line of work.

'Are we really going to wait here for that young police lady to make you tea, Daniel?'

'Nah,' I say, and I hold up the handcuffed wrist. Si gives a little bow, pops his pinky into the lock and the stupid thing finally falls off my arm. I get up and drop the golden cage on the chair. The cops'll need that as Exhibit A.

'I'd rather have a bag of chips. Let's get out of here.'

'Very good, Master Dyer,' says Si, and I wrap my coat around me, adjust my purple specs, and stroll off into the darkness.

WARSUIT 1.0
JAMES LOVEGROVE

Everything changes for Odysseus Fitch when he
arrives home to discover his father has been abducted
by terrorists. Od then discovers that his father has
been designing the most powerful weapon known to
mankind, *Warsuit 1.0.* A 7m-tall robotic exoskeleton
designed to form a permanent bond with whoever
pilots it first. And that person is Od.

Armed and dangerous, Od is now trapped in a race
against time, to save his father... and the world.

ISBN 978-1-4081-5153-2
RRP £5.99